DIFFERENT
JUST
LIKE ME

For my daughter, April, and my husband, Dean

DIFFERENT JUST LIKE ME

Lori Mitchell

Charlesbridge

I was inspired to write this book after watching my daughter develop vitiligo, a loss of pigment that presents itself as white spots all over the skin. April is just like any other kid except for her white spots. We started to think about this and realized that all people are different from one another in some way, but at the same time, we are all alike.

—L. M.

Special thanks to the people and animals who posed for this book: Michael Collier; Kaylee Scalercio; Pak Sing, Patty, and Emma Chan; Paul Wangsness; Jeannie Teague and her dog, Snuffer; Jolie Kalfaian; Dave Engel; Robert Neely; Greg LaDue; Mary Thompson; Tom Wangsness; Cat Marvis; Judy, Grant, Devon, and Paige Norris; Snip West; Andrew Wong; the cats, Pumpkin and Uncle Eddy; and of course, April and Dean.

Ever heard of the "Same and Different" game? Here's how to play: Look at the small pictures underneath the words in this story. They all have characteristics that make them the same and characteristics that make them different. For example, the fish are all the same because they swim in water and have gills and eyes. They are also different because of their colors, shapes, and sizes. See how many other same and different facts you can find in this book. For other games, a five-day lesson plan, coloring book pages, and more, visit www.differentjustlikeme.cc.

Published by Charlesbridge
85 Main Street, Watertown, MA 02472
(617) 926-0329
www.charlesbridge.com

Library of Congress Cataloging-in-Publication Data
Mitchell, Lori, 1961—
   Different just like me/Lori Mitchell
     p.   cm.
   Summary: While preparing for a visit to her grandmother, a young girl notices that, like the flowers in Grammie's garden, people who are different from one another also share similarities, and it's okay to like them all the same.
     ISBN 978-0-88106-975-4 (reinforced for library use)
     ISBN 978-1-57091-490-4 (softcover)
     ISBN 978-1-60734-220-5 (ebook pdf)
     [1. Individuality—Fiction. 2. Grandmothers—Fiction.] I. Title.
PZ7.M6933Di   1999
[E]—dc21   98-4010

Printed in Korea
(hc) 10 9 8
(sc) 15

Illustrations done in acrylic paint and graphite pencil on Arches watercolor paper
Display type and text type set in Greco, Top Hat, Braille, and Gallaudet
Color separations made by Eastern Rainbow, Derry, New Hampshire
Printed by Sung In Printing in Gunpo-Si, Kyonggi-Do, Korea
Production supervision by Brian G. Walker
Designed by Lori Mitchell

It was late Sunday night, and all I could see was the glow of my fish tank. I lay on my bed watching my fish swim around and around, and I started to hum to myself. I heard Mom just outside my door.

"April, I know you're excited, but we have a whole week ahead of us before we visit Grammie. All I want to hear now is the sound of you counting sheep." That was Mom's way of saying it was time for bed. So I fluffed my pillow, pulled up my covers, and closed my eyes. It was going to be hard to wait until Friday.

 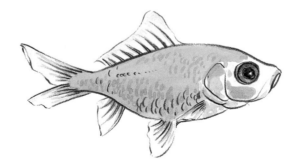 

A B C D E F G H I J K L M

On Monday morning Mom and I went into town to run errands. We got on the bus and sat across the aisle from a girl about my age. She looked at me and smiled. She was making motions with her hands, and so was her friend. Mom told me that because the girl couldn't hear, she and her friend used their hands to make words. Mom said it's a different way of talking called sign language. When we came to our stop, I waved good-bye to the girl, and she waved back, just like me.

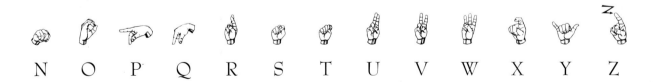

N O P Q R S T U V W X Y Z

On Tuesday we went to the farmers' market. We saw apples, plums, nectarines, and lots of fruit with names I didn't even know. There were lots of people, too. They came in all sizes, shapes, and colors. Some of them even spoke different languages. But they all liked shopping at the farmers' market, just like me.

On Wednesday we went to Dad's office to visit him. He works on the tenth floor. We rode the elevator with a lady who couldn't see. She had a friendly dog with her. Mom said the dog helped her get around. The lady found the number of her floor by feeling the little bumps beside the elevator buttons. Mom said it's a different way of reading called braille. The lady pushed her button and got off at her floor, just like me.

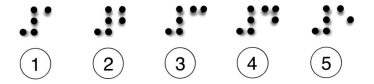

Real braille uses raised dots so that people who can't see can read by feeling the bumps.

At the ad agency where Dad works, there were people rushing everywhere. The local furniture store was having a sale, and Dad's office had to get the ads ready for the newspaper. Dad introduced me to a lady who was drawing one of the chairs that was on sale. Even though she's a grown-up, she still likes to draw, just like me.

On Thursday Mom took me out to eat at our favorite diner. I always like to sit on the stools at the counter because she lets me spin around a few times before we eat. A man came and sat down right next to me. He ordered a turkey sandwich and a glass of milk, just like me.

Before we left, I went to the rest room. While I was standing at the sink, a lady came out of the biggest stall and washed her hands. I smiled, and she said hello. She handed me a paper towel and then dried her hands, just like me.

On Friday Mom and I finally went to visit Grammie.
We had to walk down Main Street to get to the train station.

We passed tall shops, narrow shops, wide shops, and small shops. I liked looking in all the different windows.

While we waited for the train, I saw a boy standing by his mom. He was wearing a cool pirate hat.

He was going to take the number five train, just like me.

The train moved very fast. From my window I began to see lots of places I had seen before. I knew we were getting close. We hadn't seen Grammie in a long time, and I couldn't wait to give her a great big hug.

Before I knew it, Mom and I were walking down
Grammie's street. We could see Grammie's garden filled with
beautiful flowers. Grammie's neighbor, Mrs. Wong, had a
nice yard too, with red roses planted in straight rows.

But Grammie's flowers grew everywhere. There were marigolds, violets, pansies, and many other flowers in every color of the rainbow. Right in the middle of them stood Grammie, with her arms open wide, just like me.

Mrs. Wong's grandson Andrew is my friend. He always comes to see me when I visit Grammie. We had a race from Grammie's steps to the mailbox to see who could run the fastest. He's very quick, just like me.

Andrew had to go home for dinner, so Grammie's cat, Pumpkin, and I went to look at the flowers in Grammie's garden. Every time I thought I'd found my favorite, we found another one just as pretty. Grammie told me it was okay to like them all.

On Saturday night Grammie helped me pack my bag for the trip home. When I got on the train the next morning, she gave me an armful of flowers from her garden and a big hug good-bye. I sat in my seat next to Mom and looked around at all the other people.

It made me think about everyone we had seen over the last week: the girl on the bus, the shoppers in the market, the man in the diner, and the others. Like the flowers in Grammie's garden, they were all different from one another, and that's what made them so great. I'm glad everyone is different . . . just like me!